To Nathew. Enjoy! JR

Patrick the Pooping

Sponsored by:

Cambridgeshire
Catering & Cleaning Services

Providing healthier meals for over 200 schools across Cambridgeshire, Essex, Peterborough and Northamptonshire
Encouraging and promoting the health and well-being of the communities we serve.

Thanks to the inspiration from the pupils of Terrington St. John in Wisbech, and those pesky pelicans in Tortola...

www.montaguepublishing.co.uk

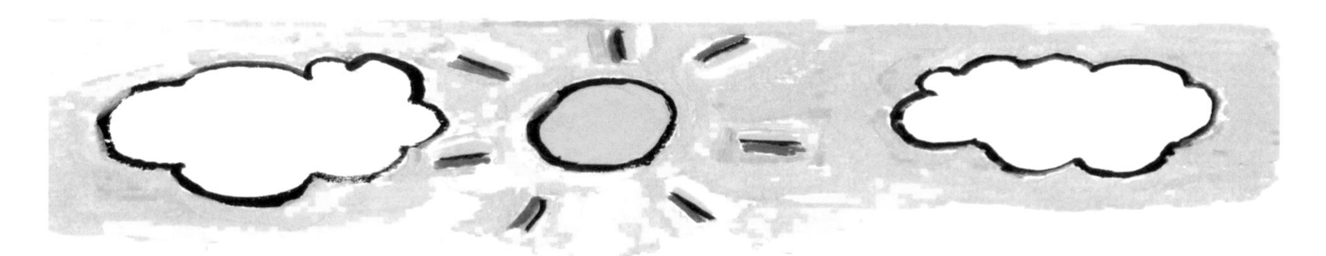

As the blazing sun shone down on the small friendly Caribbean island of Tortola, an egg in a nest began to move. It wobbled to the left, it wobbled to the right. Then a tiny crack began to appear down its smooth side. The crack spread slowly down the egg's side and a tiny beak poked out, gulping in fresh air. A little pair of sky-blue eyes blinked and peered out of the shell. Little did they know what a strange and amusing tale had begun...

A small girl called Pollyanna sat on the beach and looked out to sea. She saw surfers riding behind the crests of white waves and waved at her father on his board. He smiled back and beckoned her into the water, but she shook her head. She much preferred being on the sand. Leaving her towel behind she began to explore the beach. She laughed as she heard music coming from the café on the beach; a loud song about Santa in the Caribbean. She bounced on the soft white sand at the back of Josiah's Bay and avoided the spiky sand grass that grew up like scarecrow's arms.

Suddenly, Pollyanna stopped. There in the very corner of the beach, sitting in a hollow in the sand was a nest woven from sand grass and twigs. Two scruffy looking beach dogs were furiously pawing at the nest. “Hey you...get out...get out!” she screamed at the dogs. Both mutts looked up with their mouths full of pale lime eggs.
“Go on...get out!” she yelled and threw a stick at them.

Pollyanna looked at the devastated nest.
"Poor babies," she sighed.
But just as she began to turn to leave, she spotted something light brown and fluffy under the nest. She carefully lifted the nest and a funny looking thing with beautiful eyes and a beak that was way too big for him looked back at her.
Hearing a sharp bark from behind her, she turned to see the mangy looking beach dogs had returned.
"They're not getting you!" she said firmly. She gently picked up the strange little bird and put him in her sun hat and carried him back to the beach.

Pollyanna told her
father everything that had
happened and he agreed that
it wasn't safe to leave the
little bird on the beach. She
took him home and made a
nest from old t-shirts in an
old wooden chest.

She fed him on milk using one of her
baby sister's milk bottles.

"I will call him Patrick!" she smiled.

As Patrick grew and grew, the people of Road Town got used to the familiar sight of Patrick being pulled into town on an old wooden cart.
“Morning Patrick!” smiled Farmer Winston one day.
“Morning Winston!” gulped Patrick.
“When are you going to teach him to fly?” asked Winston.

"He's right you know Patrick," smiled Pollyanna looking into his large round eyes. "You do need to fly."
Patrick nodded his head and opened his beak making his funny gulping noise.
"Will you teach me to fly?" Patrick asked.
Pollyanna took him to the beach and gently placed him on a crumbling white wall.
"Right flap your wings like this and jump," she said, flapping her arms wildly up and down.
Patrick gulped and flapped his wings as hard as he could and then jumped, but fell beak first into the sand.

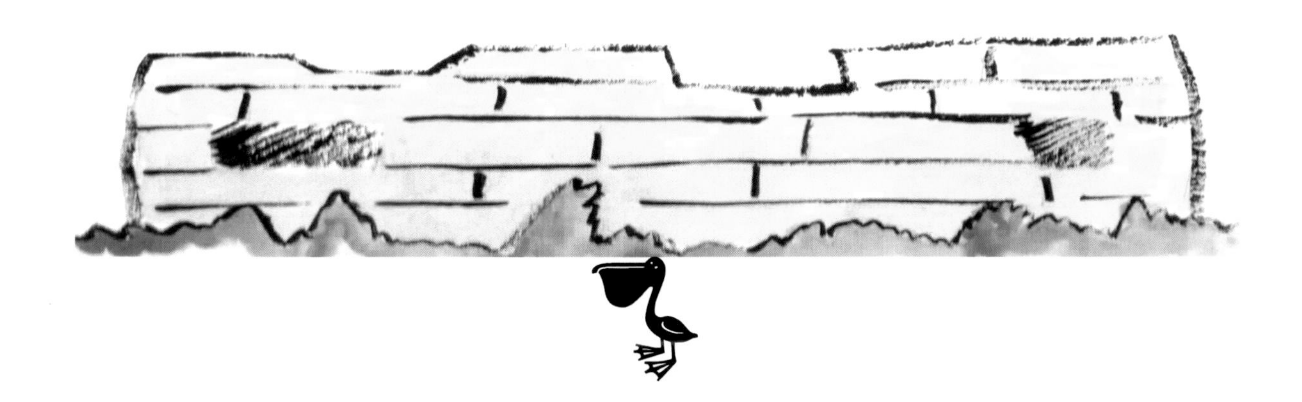

But Pollyanna never gave up. Day after day she would take him to the beach and flap her arms wildly. They often got very strange looks from the cruise ship tourists. Finally, one day Patrick beat his wings furiously and as he jumped, he soared into the sky. Pollyanna whooped in delight as he clumsily flapped and swooped. He flew over Road Town and the people smiled and clapped, but little did they know what was to come..

As his confidence grew Patrick began flying over Road Town and the surrounding areas, waving and shouting to his friends. One morning he flapped his wings and set off. He followed the line of the shore and giggled as he saw his reflection in the water. The sea looked as inviting as a bowlful of jelly, so he dived in, cooling himself in the water. He decided to go and see his friend Farmer Winston, so he took off again.

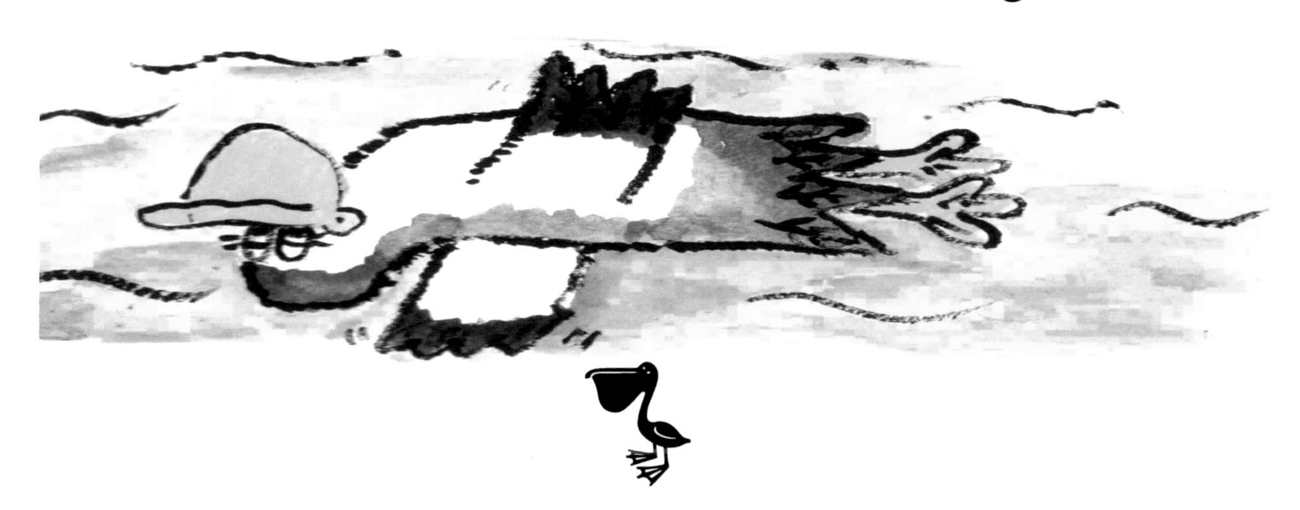

As he neared Winston's farm he could see the farmer digging a crop of plantain in the field.
"Morning Winston!" Patrick shouted.
"Morning Patrick," Winston replied, waving and leaning on his spade.
Seeing that his friend was busy, Patrick began to leave. Then a strange thing happened. Patrick got a very funny feeling in his tummy. It felt like it was going round and round like a washing machine and before he could stop, his tummy squeezed and with horror Patrick dropped something nasty from the air. He could only watch in horror as his poop bomb plumeted towards Farmer Winston, landing on the poor farmer's arm.

Farmer Winston looked up in shock. Poor Parick went red with embarassment. "Patrick Pelican please stop pooping on me!" shouted the farmer waving his fist.

Shouting that he was terribly sorry, Patrick flew away. He usually had such good manners and was really upset with what he'd done. He decided that he should head for home.

He soon realised he was over the local school. The children in the playground got really excited and began to wave at Patrick. Feeling a little better about himself, Patrick hovered around smiling at the children. He could see their friendly teacher, Miss Freemont, in the playground sitting on a bench drinking her tea. Suddenly it began to happen again. Patrick felt his tummy begin to go all funny and before he could stop himself he pooped again!
The children pointed as Patrick's missiles hurtled towards their teacher. They zoomed through the sky and with a plop landed in Miss Freemont's teacup!

Poor Miss Freemont didn't notice the special delivery in her tea and took a big sip! "Eeeerrrggghhh...!" she spluttered as she spat out her tea. The children pointed up to the sky and explained to their teacher what had happened. "Patrick Pelican, please stop pooping on me!" she shouted, waving her mug of tea angrily.

“I’m sorry...I didn’t mean to!” cringed poor Patrick as he flew off ashamed. He really wanted this to stop. As fast as he could, he flew for home. He hoped that Pollyanna would be able to help him. He reached the edge of Road Town and slowed down to catch his breath. He could see Tessa the hairdresser outside her shop. She was famous for her wonderfully elegant hairstyles. “Oh no...not again!” cried Patrick as he felt that now familiar feeling in his tummy.

Knowing what was coming he quickly shouted from the air. “Watch out, watch out! Cover your beautiful hair!” But it was too late...his unwanted gift rocketed towards Tessa and landed straight in her marvellous hair!

Tessa let out a shrill scream as she felt something splat on her head. She looked up at Patrick in disgust. "Patrick Pelican, please stop pooping on me!" she wailed, running into her shop to fix her hair.

Patrick was distraught. Crying huge tears he flapped for home, unable to understand what was happening. This popular and friendly bird had become public enemy number one. He flew home and frantically banged on Pollyanna's window. She rushed out to see what was wrong. Patrick sobbed and sobbed. He told her all about what had happened.

“Everybody hates me!” he cried. “There’s something wrong with me!”

Pollyanna sat down and gave Patrick a hug.
She scratched her head and thought really hard.
“What did you eat for breakfast?” she asked.
“Mango, from the trees in the garden,” he replied.
“And what did you have for lunch?” she asked.
“Bananas from the field,” he replied.
“And yesterday?“ she asked.
“Mangoes, bananas and passion fruit. It’s what I eat everyday,” he answered a little confused.

"Oh Patrick you silly bird," she smiled.
"There's nothing wrong with you...you're just eating too much fruit!"
"Is fruit bad for you?" he asked.
"Of course not, in fact it's really good for you. It's just that you can't eat *only* fruit. You have to have a balanced diet; a little bit of all types of food. Let's teach you to fish and I promise you, your smelly little problem will go away."

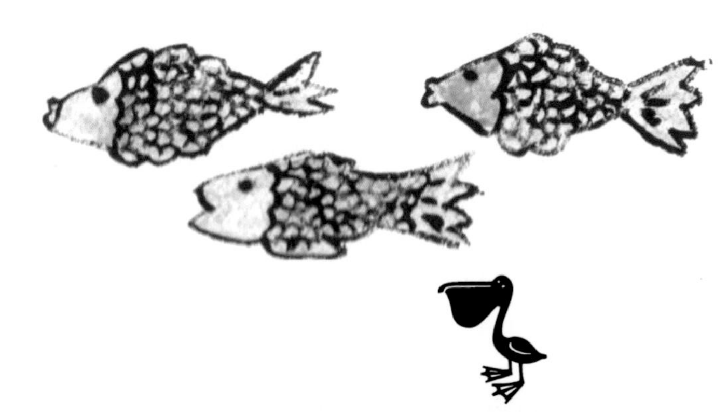

A few days later, Patrick took to the skies again. Farmer Winston looked up to see Patrick flapping towards him. He ran to hide under the shelter of a tamarind tree, but Patrick waved and shouted with a caw,"Patrick Pelican is not pooping no more!"

As Miss Freemont watched the children playing, she spotted a shadow hovering on the playground. She quickly covered her tea with her hand, but Patrick waved and shouted with a caw,
"Patrick Pelican is not pooping no more!"

Tessa the hairdresser was opening her shop, when she saw a pelican reflected in the window. She covered her hair with a newspaper, but Patrick waved and shouted with a caw,
"Patrick Pelican is not pooping no more!"
Patrick was once again the most popular bird in town...

...but everyone has to go
to the toilet sometimes!!

THE
PELICAN
SONG

CHORUS

LOOK UP TO THE SKY,
YOU BETTER WATCH OUT,
'COS PATRICK IS COMING,
EVERYBODY WILL SHOUT,
LOOK UP TO THE SKY,
SEE HIS BEAUTIFUL WINGS,
HERE COMES PATRICK,
BRINGING SMELLY TINGS!

On a small, friendly isle in the Caribbean,
A strange and amusing tale had begun,
A girl found a pelican and called him Parick,
He grew really tame and he grew really quick,
Patrick he became a familiar sight,
Flying over village in morning and night,
The people would wave "It's Patrick!" they said,
And everyone smiled, till he pooped on their head!

CHORUS

It started one day as he flew and he glided,
“I’ll go and see Winston,” Patrick decided,
He beat his wings and he swooped through the sky,
To shout down to Winston as he circled by.
Farmer Winston was planting a crop,
As Patrick flew over a poop he did drop,
Winston looked up and he shouted a plea,
“Patrick Pelican please stop pooping on me!”

CHORUS

He carried on flying and looked all around,
He saw Miss Fremont in the playground,
The children all shouted and yelled out in glee,
But they were all shocked when he pooped in her tea,
Miss Fremont was waving and missed the big drip.
She lifted the mug and she took a big sip,
She shouted “That’s nasty!” and spat out the tea,
“Patrick Pelican please stop pooping on me!”

CHORUS

As Patrick flew home he passed a hairdresser,
Owned by a talented woman called Tessa,
He flew by at speed and he looked down there,
And saw a fine lady with curls in her hair,
"Look out!" Patrick shouted from up in the air,
"Put your hands over your beautiful hair!"
Too late, out came poop number three,
She said "Patrick please stop pooping on me!"

CHORUS

He found Pollyanna and said "Something's awry,
I keep on pooping from up in the sky!"
"Oh Patrick you really are cute,
"You've just been eating way too much fruit!"
"No fruit in your bowl, no peach in your dish,
"We need to go out and teach you to fish!"
He flew back to his friends and he said with a caw,
"Patrick Pelican is not pooping *no more*!"

CHORUS

TO FIND OUT MORE ABOUT THE PATRICK THE PELICAN AND OTHER WORKS BY JON BRIDGEMAN CHECK OUT...

www.montaguepublishing.co.uk

AND FIND THE PELICAN SONG ON YOU TUBE AT:

http://www.youtube.com/watch?v=fuqQfxFno-c

AND THE GINGERBREAD RAP ON YOU TUBE AT:

http://www.youtube.com/watch?v=Mv1jDwnH7mk

About the Author

Jon Bridgeman started writing for children in 2001. He has written many short stories, poems and is still writing his 'masterpiece' a fantasy novel for children. Patrick the Pooping Pelican is his third published book. Jon's ideas and inspiration come from years spent as a classroom teacher and reading stories to children. 'If it makes me laugh...it normally makes them giggle too!'

About the Illustrator

Rachel Cooper is a busy artist, teacher and mum! She began drawing children's books at university and continued drawing when she began teaching. Stranded on a Caribbean island in 2003 with no books to teach with she began drawing and making her own books. She is delighted that years of practice have finally seen her drawings in print.